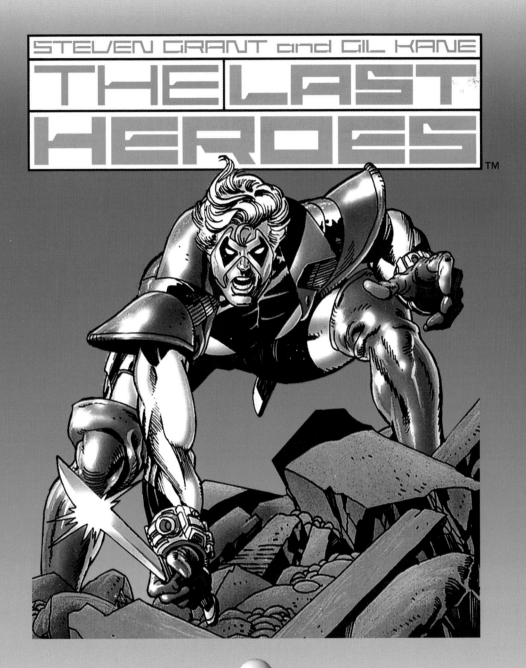

STEVEN GRANT and GIL KANE
THE LAST HEROES ™

ibooks

NEW YORK
www.ibooks.net

DISTRIBUTED BY SIMON & SCHUSTER, INC.

A Publication of ibooks, inc.

Editorial Note:
The superhero team The Ultimates and the character of Mr. Ultimate, as depicted in this
graphic novel, are creations of Steven Grant and Gil Kane, and were originally conceived in
1993. They are in no way meant to represent any characters or situations currently
appearing in the similarly-titled comic book series *The Ultimates* published by Marvel
Entertainment Group.

ibooks, inc.
24 West 25th Street
New York, NY 10010

The ibooks World Wide Web site Address is:
http://www.ibooks.net

The ibooks Graphic Novels Web site Address is:
http://www.komikwerks.com

ISBN: 0-7434-9321-4
First ibooks, inc. printing: October 2004
10 9 8 7 6 5 4 3 2 1

Cover art by Gil Kane

Printed in Spain by Norma Editorial

Introduction

In the beginning was Gil Kane.

For me, anyway. In 1961, I was a sick little kid suffering through a week of mumps or some such childhood disease when my dad bought a copy of DC Comics' *All-Star Western* to amuse me. Gil was already almost two decades into his career as a comics artist, having worked his way up from the mean streets of Brooklyn, via apprenticeships with various artists back when such a thing was common, to key artist for one of the key editors of the era, Julius Schwartz. After all that time, and scores of stories, he was just beginning to make a jump to status of premier artist, courtesy of a superhero comic called *Green Lantern*. Among the other things he drew was "Johnny Thunder," the lead feature in *All-Star Western*. I didn't know it at the time.

But it had a profound effect on my taste in comics art. Almost all the comics I liked the best turned out to be drawn by Gil Kane. Once I found that out, Gil was it.

Gil's influence on comics art was huge. He redefined action art in the '60s and '70s, creating a whole new language that dozens of other artists picked up on and mixing a new degree of tension with the refined physical beauty an artist named Lou Fine had brought to comics in the 1940s, but which hadn't been very prominent since. He specialized in kinetic motion; by the mid-'60s there wasn't a character he drew who didn't look like their bodies housed tightly compressed coiled springs. Often battling editorial preference, he constantly sought the most exciting angles for his shots and more often than not found them. When one of his characters threw a punch, you felt the impact. He showed a generation of comics artists how to do it.

Then he moved over to Marvel Comics and really cut loose. In the meantime he kept trying to generate new formats and content and widen the range of possibility for comics, including arguably the first modern American graphic novel, the violent spy thriller *His Name is... Savage*, published in magazine form, and the paperback barbarian adventure serial *Blackmark*.

Meanwhile I grew up. I came to appreciate many other comics artists. But Gil was always it for me. Even now, several years after his death, it still is.

I almost worked with him several times. As a writer at Marvel in the late '70s, shortly after breaking into the business, I was hired on several occasions to write stories specifically for Gil to draw. I did. They didn't know it, but I would have done them for free. I'm glad I didn't. Every one of them got assigned to other artists instead.

It's funny the odd little dreams we end up with. I didn't know it until then, but one of my big career dreams was to have one of my stories drawn by Gil Kane. By the mid-'80s, Gil had moved, temporarily, into animation and Los Angeles, though he still kept his hand in comics. I'd also moved to Los Angeles. By a quirk of fate, we ended up living half a block away from each other. But he didn't know me from a hole in the wall, and every time I considered hitting his buzzer and blathering, "Uh, Mr. Kane, you don't know me but I write comics and I've loved your work since I was seven," I could hear myself saying and thought, "This is a good way to get arrested."

So we never met then either. Call it cowardice, but I knew my dream of working with Gil Kane was never going to happen.

Flash forward another eight years. By then I lived in the Pacific Northwest, and had an agent/lawyer named Harris Miller, who also repped Frank Miller (no relation), Howard Chaykin, and a number of other comics artists and writers. This was a flush time, when a number of popular artists left Marvel Comics and banded together to form a company called Image Comics, which briefly operated through another company called Malibu Comics before going off on their own. That venture left Malibu flush with cash and ready to cash in on the boom market, starting with their Ultraverse line of superheroes. Meanwhile, Harris convinced them to run a boutique label of creator-owned comics—it was ultimately called Bravura—for his clients. Malibu was hot for it. It was an exciting time.

One day I get a phone call from Harris. "Would you consider creating a book for Gil to draw?"

Ever had one of those *Twilight Zone* moments where you wonder if you'd just wandered into some strange alternate universe?

It turned out to be a bit gosh-wow embarrassing for a little while after that, as I churned out all the things I'd decided not to say over Gil's intercom years before. He was nice enough to put up with it. Then we got to what we should do.

It may come as a shock to many familiar with Gil's work, but he was never very fond of superheroes. He felt nothing interesting was usually said with them, that most stories ignored the essential tensions of the concept, as well as the underlying mythic quality. Still, it's what he was associated with, and, given that superheroes were burning up the stands in those days, what Gil felt we ought to produce for maximum initial impact. I wasn't all that keen on superheroes myself at the time, and especially not keen on trying to come up with something that hadn't been done with them before. This was in the wake of breakthrough material like Alan Moore and Dave Gibbons' *Watchmen* and Frank Miller's *Dark Knight Returns*, which, between them, seemed on the surface to open new possibilities but really burned them out.

We talked. And talked. And talked. Gil, if nothing else, was a born raconteur, spitting out wonderful stories of his life in the business with every other breath, and a born idea man. At this point I have no idea who came up with what, we batted ideas back and forth so much and so quickly, but eventually the concept and story took shape. Alan Moore in particular, in *Watchmen* and *Marvelman*, pioneered the examination of the effect of superheroes in a "real" world, and I felt once introduced that notion couldn't be walked away from. (Though many have done it since.) In addition, we needed that mythic tone Gil desired. By the time we were done—I won't reiterate it, since you can flip forward a few pages to see what happened—we had wrapped a story around an evolutionary tract, set a group of superheroes in a world where there were no supervillains (at least not apparently), and left huge questions as to who was actually the hero and the villain of the story. We called it *Edge*, after Gil wisely rejected my initial suggestion of *Slaughter*. (An intended homage to real-life western marshal Blackjack Slaughter.) We intended it to be both a fun action story and a nasty little examination of the generally accepted unconscious precepts of the superhero genre. It wasn't long before it came out.

Just long enough.

By the time *Edge* was published, the '90s comics craze bubble had burst. Revenues were plummeting. As comics went, *Edge* was fairly successful. Just not successful enough to justify the ridiculous sums Malibu was paying us per our Harris Miller-negotiated contracts. Gil was just putting the finish on the fourth issue art when we were notified it would never be published. Bravura was kaput.

It was a huge disappointment. *Edge* had been conceived as three four-issue miniseries. Bad enough the other two arcs wouldn't appear, but fans shouldn't have been cheated of the first arc's conclusion (though it doesn't end as anyone would expect). We shopped it around, but no one wanted to publish just the one issue and it was felt too soon to reprint the first three. Gil had been sick with cancer the whole time we'd been doing it. The timing just wasn't right. *Edge* was dead.

A decade on. Gil finally lost his fight with cancer; it's a sadder world without him. To my surprise, the ideas we put forth in *Edge* were never duplicated elsewhere, what we had planned still hasn't been done by anyone else. Faced with a new publisher, a new series name, another chance to get it right and maybe even to tell those lost stories and more, I can look at this work and see vast veins of gold waiting to be mined here, things so obvious to both of us that no one else ever said, and, strangely, the promise of new life for a genre that not long ago I thought was played out.

Somehow I can hear Gil saying in my ear with a creator's pride, "My boy, I knew this day would come."

Gil, this one's for you.

—Steven Grant

SELF-DEFENSE, HE'LL INSIST LATER. INSTINCT.

CONVULSIONS: THE WHIP CRACKS. A BODY SNAPS ONE WAY, TOWARD A ROOFTOP, THE OTHER INTO OPEN AIR.

HE DIDN'T WANT THIS.

A MOMENT OF HORROR.

TWO POINTS. DISTINCT. DISCONNECTED.

A FROZEN MOMENT. AN ANGEL, SUSPENDED BY PERCEPTION. THE CITY IS DEAD OF SOUND.

SOME ELEMENTS WILL RESIST: THE SILENCE, THE FEAR.

HE REMEMBERS FEAR, AND SILENCE. MEMORY IS HIS CURSE.

HE KNOWS SOMETHING OF HORROR.

IT WILL FADE. MEMORY WILL REWORK AND RECON- STRUCT IT INTO NECESSITY.

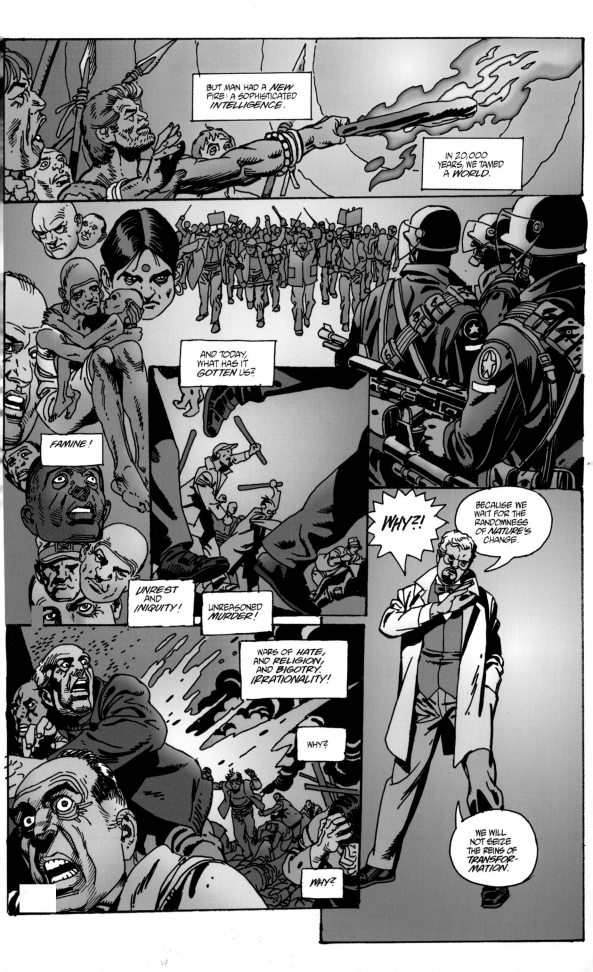

OUTSIDE THE OFFICIAL STORY SPREADS, BUT WORD ON THE STREET MOVES QUICKER:

"AN ULTIMATE HAS BEEN MURDERED!"

A TANK LIKE HIS MADE ULTIMATES. HE CAN MAKE ULTIMATES.

HE CAN BE AN ULTIMATE!

A POWER! A MYTH!

NOT THE FIRST TIME, HE KNOWS. HIDDEN. THINKING.

NOT THE LAST, HE FEARS.

HE HAS LIVED IT ALL BEFORE.

PERSEUS! BEOWULF! ST. GEORGE!

THE WHEEL COMES ROUND, CYCLES OF HOPE AND DEATH.

A HERO!

HE WONDERS HOW TO BREAK THE CYCLE.

ERIC CARNELL-- EDGE--FIGHTING MONSTERS!

THE WHEEL

TO BE CONTINUED...

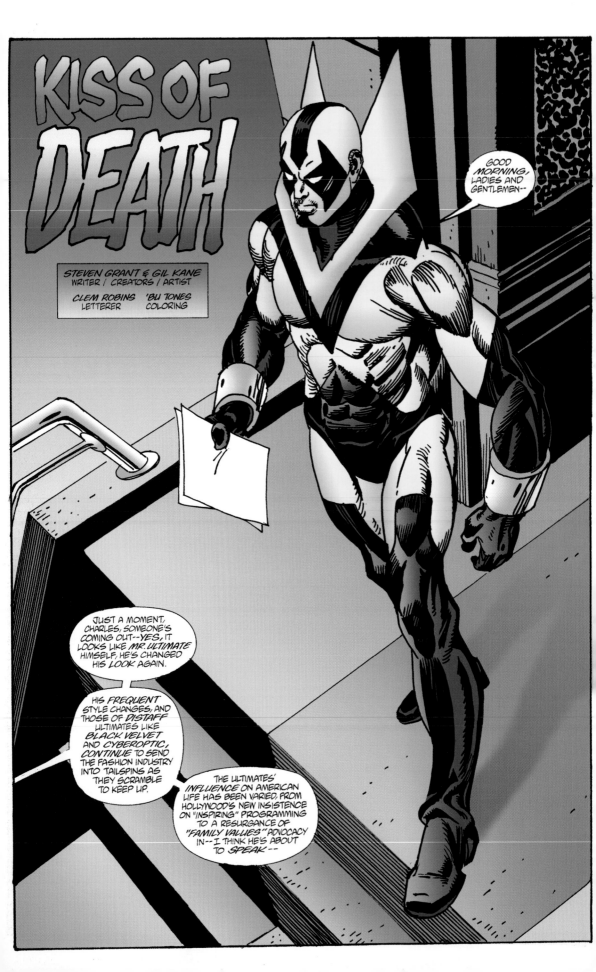

AS SHE PASSES, WOMEN VANISH INTO SHADOWS AND DOORWAYS.

MEN CLUSTER, BREATHLESS, AT ARM'S LENGTH.

SHE PRETENDS NOT TO NOTICE.

THIS IS HOW, AT NINE, SHE DREAMED LIFE WOULD BE.

REVOLVING AROUND HER.

BLACK VELVET!

BILLY! NICE OUTFIT.

NEW?

MORE OF BENNETT'S CRAP. YOU'D KNOW THAT IF YOU'D BEEN AT THE MEETING.

WHERE THE HELL WERE YOU?! WE WERE AFRAID THIS EDGE IMPOSTER GOT YOU!

WHAT?! ARE YOU ALL RIGHT?

OH, HE GOT ME.

CALM DOWN, HE'S JACK'S BROTHER. I USED TO BE ENGAGED TO HIM.

IF I TELL YOU WHERE HE IS, WILL YOU TAKE HIM DOWN QUICKLY? WITHOUT HURTING HIM? HE'S NOT REALLY BAD...

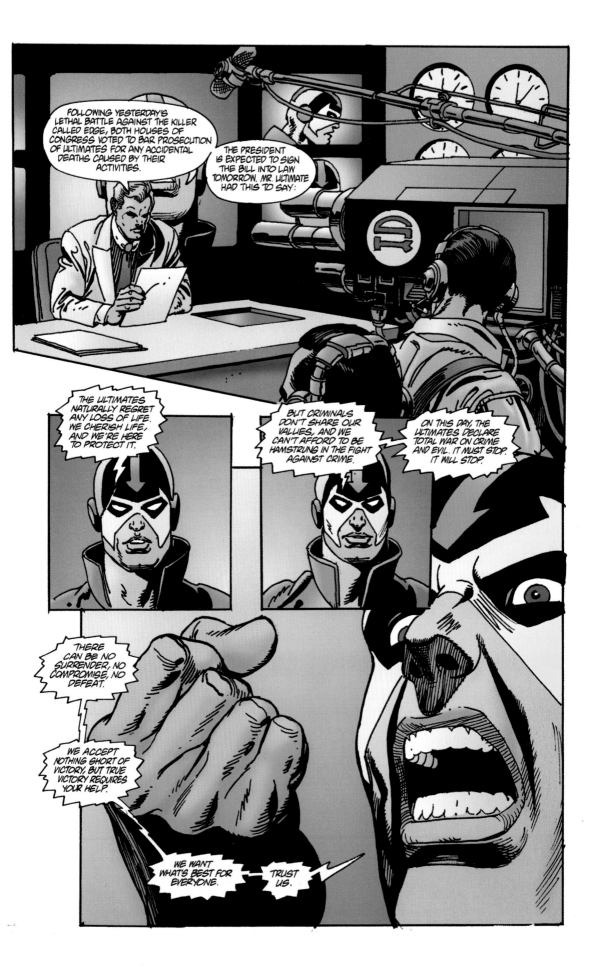

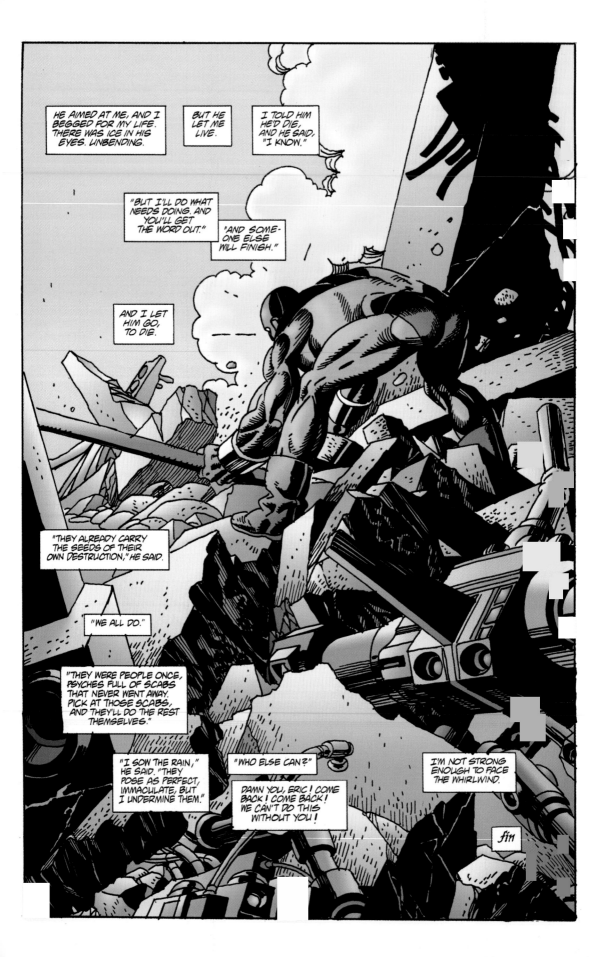

Created by

STEVEN GRANT & GIL KANE

Written by

STEVEN GRANT

Artwork by

GIL KANE

Color Design by

LYDIA NOMURA

FALLING FROM GRACE

A vignette of the First EDGE™

An old brownstone, rotting in the shadow of skyscrapers. Burning. Flames lick from every window, smoke sends children and firemen running for air. No one has cared about this building, this neighborhood, these people in years. Fire hoses spit water, but spit would do as much. From the building, a streak, passing in a blink so fast even those rescued, screaming, don't see him.

Into the building, searching for victims with brutal, impatient kindness: Mr Ultimate.

—-What's the situation? The young one, in white leather, swaggering of toughness and purity: Edge.

The blur stops, rigid, solid, Supersonic, muscles twitching, shimmering, still moving, still fighting to move. —-Drug lab's up in fire, think we caught then all, but anyone hiding will be crispy by now.

—-As far as we can tell, all the civilians made it. Overhead, a gliding hiss, the shadow of wings: Winged Victory.

A fireman charges out, rubber coat smoldering, a stink worse than the smoke. Damped by the rain. —-It's coming apart! Best we can do now is contain it! Supersonic lurches, Edge catches his chest, holding him back from the flames.

—-We can't all put our lives at risk. You help out here. I'm leader, I'll find Bennett.

And he's gone, in flames, vanished into the building, ignoring frantic

shouts:

——You're no more fireproof than we are!

A reply he hopes someone heard as the fire snaps at him and the world burns away into a smoky orange haze: ——But I'm leader.

His electric corona, the expression of his power holds the fire at bay, but the heat burns away his air. Choking, ——Bennett! Let's go! The place is collapsing!

——Figured you'd come, Jack. You look hot. He turns, air ripples. A burning doorway, a smoky silhouette beyond. The shadow snaps at him, closer than he thought, something cracks in his jaw and pure white light bursts behind Edge's eyes. The voice is mirage, distant. ——It's all in the mind, you know. Think of ice cubes.

——Bennett?

——Bennett. Bennett bennett bennett bennett bennett. Standing over him now, Edge up on one knee, fumbling for concentration. The corona gone, lost with his focus. His vest on fire. No sympathy in the dark, hovering face. ——Don't call me that. My name's Mr. Ultimate.

——That's no...A kick catches his chest, throws him back. Cinders where he lands, red-hot burning black, ash fluttering on waves of heat.

——I've had enough of you and your father. I'm taking over. The heat shadow lunges toward him, smelling blood. A pulse circuits through him, electric, sucking charge from skin, hair, guts, everything, all the voltage he has stored, static and stolen, his eyes spark and his hands are burning, pointing...

——Like hell!

The shadow erupts white, crackling. And laughs, singed but unhurt.

His mouth hangs open, unable to close, blood runs from his nose. The shadow still crackles, brief sparks flitting off, dying in the fire. He's on fire, his legs and back, the vest gone, but nerves are dead, brain numb, energy wasted.

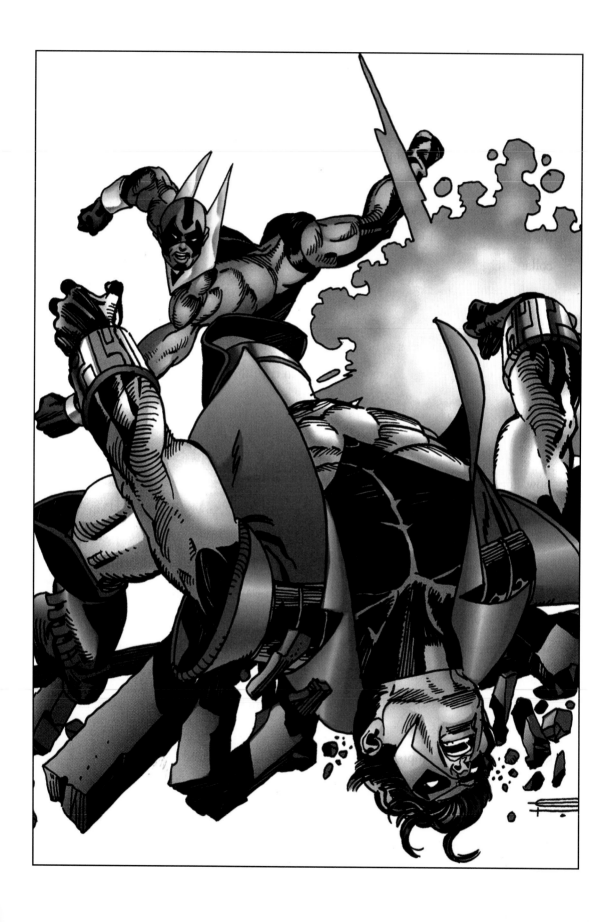

—You and Daddy never understood, Jack. you've got to go, you're impediments now. These powers you gave us, did you think they were random? He tries to push himself up, tries to feel his hands. The floor too hot to touch. Sprawled on it, burning. —When you tested on convicted murderers, you couldn't suppose their self-images would be monstrous?

—How...? He finds his voice, a smoky rasp. —...did you know about The Plague?

The shadow, Bennett, who had been an ally, ignores him. Edge, already dead. To him. —Is it by chance a man who wanted to fly grew wings? That a track star became the fastest being on earth? Where's your altruistic crap, Jack, how does your glowing help the poor and hungry? Lifting him by the wrists, his toy, ruined now, lost to the fire. Pustules on his cracking lips, skin stripped raw with heat, Bennett's plaything, already thrown away. —Know what you wanted to be, Jack? A superstar!

—You're wrong...

—Really? Then why all the parties, all the women? That's what you wanted: the fun, the popularity, the respect. Fifty years of your father's work, so you could get girls...The hand strikes violently, unexpectedly, with casual grace, snapping him from the void of pain, to listen. —Such anemic lusts, such anemic powers. Know what I wanted? The only thing on my mind?

And he wants to know before he dies, he knows death is coming, he doesn't understand it but he can't crawl away, too much broken inside, too much skin burned away, too much fire everywhere. Bennett's words stretch to years, he has to center to grasp them, if he stays centered he doesn't die, doesn't go away, but where did it go, it's gone...

—It's what you're up against...The voice soft now, untouched by fire. —Pure power, and the brains to use it properly. I'm the best, Jack. The ultimate. And I didn't become this to kowtow to your old man or take orders from you. I

didn't do it to save the world. That's your problem, you thought powers would change the world. You think with your powers. Powers are just self-gratification. Gimmicks. Power changes the world.

The drone balloons, fading, too comforting, he's overloaded, circuits blown, pain shuts him off...

—-The next generation of Ultimates will conform to my specifications. Maybe the next generation of the world...Strong hands on his neck, twisting, a snap and he's free, gone...

The room seethes blue. Where they were born, in the tanks. Heavy footsteps in the hallway, but the old man doesn't raise his head. Doesn't look as they enter. The radio is switched off now. He can't catch his breath.

—-I'm...sorry...we...were cleaning out a neighborhood of crack houses...there was a fire... no one was with him...We didn't know what happened until...

A hand raised, stern, a gesture cutting him off. —-It's not Jack. A sideways glance. The shape is red, dirty, blackened in patches. Not his son.

—-Sir?

—-What did you do to him, Bennett?

—-Sir?

—-Jack had powers! He...! Nothing could have...! Drymouthed, he can't catch his breath. —-He was careful! He knew what he was doing! Bennett hides his face, the thing on the floor still hot in the cool of the Institute, the corpse of a dream.

—-Just go away...just go away...

Afterword

There's a recurring gimmick in superhero comics, courtesy of science fiction, based on the fact that we use only one-tenth of our brains at any given time. This is translated, in comic books, into using only one-tenth of our intellectual potential or "brainpower"— such is how language twists meaning—with the correlate that if we could only tap the other 90% of that power, our full potential, we would become like unto gods. Or super-men.

But brain activity is measured by how many little sparks of electricity jump from one synapse to the another in our nervous systems, telling our bodies which muscles to move, etc. At any given time, roughly 10% of our synapses are firing. 100% brain activity would mean 100% of our synapses would be firing all the time. Which would put every muscle in the body in a state of full tension all the time. Which would effectively result in total paralysis. It would be like sticking your finger in a light socket and keeping it there. One hell of a superpower, innit?

Things like that prompted Gil and me to create the book you just read.

As I mentioned in the introduction, Gil was never particularly fond of superheroes, but that was less a fondness of the concept and more a disdain for what was done with it. Despite their strong science fiction under-pinnings, the two DC Comics characters with which he's most strongly associated, Green Lantern and The Atom, were, like all DC's characters, basically suburban heroes. Despite their powers and the wonder of the milieu they frequented, their interests and personalities were mundane. Their stories mostly ran in 8-16 pages. The good guys were the good guys and the bad guys were the bad guys, and, in most cases, that was as nuanced as they got.

Gil wanted more complex things. Opera, and the raw vitality of the pulps. Human emotion. A sense of mythology.

Then there was my pet peeve about superheroes: the moral certainty of the genre. For a long time, I'd played up moral ambiguity in superhero stories to the extent my publishers would allow it, which usually wasn't much. It always seemed to me there was a huge amount of ambiguity built into the whole concept of superheroes, glossed over mostly by looking the other way. You get superpowers, you put on a costume and do good deeds. (Like Spider-Man, you might experience a little duress at first, but then you get into it.) Yeah, that sure sounds like the way it would happen in the real world.

Superheroes in the "real" world was something we were forced (not unwillingly) to tackle. Most superhero books these days are set on worlds where such things are common-place. Since we were flying solo, we didn't have that luxury. It became a central issue: every environment has its own ecology, and the intrusion of any outside element upsets that ecology, often unexpectedly. Like "superheroes" plopped in the real world. The commonplace in superhero comics is for the superhero to arise parallel or in response to the supervillain. But what if there were no supervillains? What on earth does the world need supermen for when there are no threats capable of challenging them?

Which is why, in the first chapter, the Ultimacy is first seen strikebreaking. It's a traditional role for the forces of "law and order," but one which, with sympathetic opponents, put their own moral superiority in doubt. What's more "super"? To uphold law and order or side with the underdog? What kind of role would supermen have in our world? Besides being the gaudy equivalent of pop stars?

Then there's the question of evolution. At least as far back as Nietzsche, the "super-man" is expected to be the next evolutionary jump. It's an idea absorbed whole into super-hero comics, rarely questioned, and accept-ed as right and proper, a boon to mankind. The notion that you can somehow jumpstart evolution (our science on this was probably as sound as gobbledygook is likely to get, but we had to have some conceits)—and that such a thing is inherently good—became our rationale for why the Ultimacy is created, and I had great fun writing James Carnell's stirring orientation speech about the inher-ent nobility of such a purpose. It stands in marked contrast to what the Ultimacy actu-ally manages to accomplish within the four issues and, like most superhero comics, it intentionally overlooks the great unknown in the equation: the people being transformed are still people, filled with doubts, cravings and neuroses. (If there's anything I regret about this arc, it's not having the room to play more with the character Narcissus, who was intended to be a pivotal character, the team's unacknowledged resident psychopath, consciencelessly capable, as more and more power accrues to the Ultimacy, of increasingly horrible things.)

What superhero comics ignore in Nietzsche was the second half of his equation. The superman is not coming to, as James Carnell supposes, fix the world on behalf of the human race. Nietzsche's superman is coming to *replace* the human race. Mr. Ultimate accepts that as a given: if they're the next evolutionary step, then they're the next evolutionary step, and whatever their *intended* purpose, the logical implications take precedent. It's hard to get more unequivocal than that. Before the Ultimacy arises, Dr. Carnell's dreams, driven without acknowledgment by his own cravings and neuroses, take precedent, but once they're created the only thing that matters is what *the Ultimacy* wants.

If the members of the Ultimacy are our heirs to the Greek heroes, Edge, one of their trinity of creators (the other two having been killed in Nietzschean fashion), is potentially the god who can crush them, but he's also Victor Frankenstein facing off against the monster who has gone beyond his control. He is the agent of evolution, who we chose to attack another cherished myth of comics, that evolution is a continuum aiming toward destiny. In that egocentric view, the superhuman is the natural future of humanity. But that isn't how evolution works. It's a messy, sloppy process, filled with far more failures than successes. What Edge posits—that the Ultimacy isn't "the next step" but evolutionary dead ends, for the reasons he cites—is more than just a philosophy, it's a statistical likelihood. (Not to mention an editorial comment.) But Edge also plays up the ambiguity of the series; for all the weight his status of underdog loner gives his viewpoint—another tradition in comics—there's no guarantee anywhere in the story that he's right. Mr. Ultimate may, by the end of this arc, clearly not be a good guy, but, read the right way, Edge may not be either.

Whatever. As you know by now (if you haven't read the book yet, read it and come back when you're done) Edge has a bad time at arc's end; while he may be philosophically correct in the long run, he's, ah, *ulti-*mately* outmatched in the short run. This might seem like a logical, if not particularly satisfying, place to end things, which is why Gil and I ended there.

But it was never really meant to end there. Gil may no longer be with us, but I am and our ideas are. Edge makes no appearance in the next arc, which takes place a couple years after this arc. His name is never mentioned. He only factors in as a philosophical irritant, as the Ultimacy's effect on the world broadens dramatically yet their unrelenting human nature and Edge's warnings undermine their progress, and the Ultimacy is finally forced to make serious decisions about what they want the world to be.

The third arc (or act, if you'd prefer), set five years after the first, is where Edge's influence, spiritual or otherwise, is felt most strongly, and where we planned to make our final judgments on the nature of heroism.

Whether all this provides *The Last Heroes* with the operatic, mythological scope Gil wanted, I couldn't say. I hope so, but I stand too close to it, and the story itself evolved naturally: a messy, sloppy process. All I know for sure is it's the story we wanted to tell, and, like most stories, it's hard to know what's it's really about until it's over. Here the ancient Greeks raise their heads again: my own tastes in drama are very Greek. (We'll set aside the notion of Edge, and even Mr. Ultimate, as tragic hero for now.) In Greek drama, if the hero dies, it's a tragedy, and if he lives, it's a comedy. Despite the earnest trappings, I always viewed *The Last Heroes* as a comedy.

But there's only one way to find out for sure, isn't there?

—Steven Grant
May 2004